Trek to the Sea

Book 4

Print ISBN: 979-8-9997014-5-9
eBook ISBN: 979-8-9997014-2-8

Table of Contents

1. Discovery	1
2. To What Do We Give Thanks	4
3. Cave of Songs	6
4. Forked Flame	10
5. Bing's Back	13
6. Kara's Vision: The Line of Mothers	16
7. Echoes of Someone's Past	19
8. Day Three	22
9. They Are Coming	24
10. The One Beneath the Snow	27
11. The Plateau That Broke	30
12. The Fever That Speaks	33
13. The Valley of Signs	36
14. The Answer in the Ash	38
15. The Clan of the Shore	40
16. Crossing the Broken Delta	45
17. The Teeth Beneath	48
18. The Signal Fire	51
19. The Clan of Echoes	55
20. The Trial of the Salt Wind	58
21. The Salt Clan	62
22. The Marsh	66
23. The Drowned Grove	68
24. The Crossing	71
Epilogue: The First Garden	74

Chapter 1

Discovery

Joy and laughter were nearly nonexistent in this harsh world, yet in their recent gatherings, Kara sought to name it. When time and circumstances permitted, they did laugh and feel joy. She referred to those moments as, “light in the dark.”

The wolves were making a racket outside the hut when she awoke. Kara pushed the Auroch-hide door cover aside and stepped into the cold morning light. The sharp sting of frost filled her lungs as she emerged, and the satisfying crunch of snow under her boots echoed the distant yips and playful growls of her wolves. They chased a snow hare through drifts of powder, their paws kicking up flurries that sparkled in the sun like embers rising from a campfire.

Watching her wolves leap and tumble across the white expanse, Kara's heart swelled with pride and affection; she understood their wild happiness as if it were her own, feeling deeply connected to their joy and energy in the frozen dawn.

It had been a long journey to reach this high plateau. The world still held memories—beyond the mountains, beyond what may determine whether they would ever discover a range that was good for a permanent camp.

Drud struggled to greet the day, unlike Kara. Toddy and Lance ran toward the hut's opening, eager for warmth and food.

Kara watched them with a quiet smile. There hadn't been any bumps in the trail for a few days. The break felt like life's struggles were easing, if only slightly.

She stepped forward, her breath visible in the morning air. Someone approached from behind her. Drud stood beside her and took her hand for the first time in a long while. His grip was rough and certain. She didn't move away.

They all watched as the wolves chased the hare. Kara felt warm, not just from the playfulness of the wolves, but also because Drud was near.

"Will we ever see what's beyond these mountains?" she asked. "Or is the rest of the world the same?"

Drud paused, as if he were trying to remember something buried beneath the snow and silence. "Kale says there's a huge never-ending body of water beyond the last shadows. This area is located beyond the peaks, where the sun shines on everything."

Kara followed his gaze to the hut, where Kale sat drawing shapes in the frost with a stick, deep in thought. Kara was good at practical things, like tracking game, reading weather, and knowing when to move and when to wait. But Kale's mind wandered toward the mythical. He had learned much from sitting around the fire, listening to elders tell stories of those who crossed into the unknown and returned with tales about faraway waters.

The stories didn't come from maps or signs; they came from memory and myth.

Drud stepped onto a rare patch of bare ground—damp, snowless, and warmed by the sun, like a secret. Something caught his eye, partially buried, a bone. He turned it over in his hand for a long time. Man.

He inhaled. The warmth vanished.

It was a leg bone worn smooth by time. Had someone taken care to bury this man, or cast him aside violently?

The bone was as smooth as a river stone, and its silence was louder than the wolves' howls. Drud thought about whether this person had once walked among them.

He looked back at Kara and then gently placed the bone in the depression left in the ground. "Let's get the day started," he said softly; he didn't want to dwell on the worrisome implication of his find.

Chapter 2

To What do we Give Thanks

"Kara's smile widened. The smell of trout filled the air with a delicious promise—earthy and bright. As they neared the outdoor hearth, they saw that Sang had carefully arranged dried plums on a stone platter. Plums that she had carried for many days and were waiting for the right moment to display them. A gift of thanks—not to a person, but to whatever power had watched over them.

The sheep bleated softly behind them, adding a musical quality to a morning ritual that felt both familiar and new. This day resembled those before it, but everyone sensed something was different, for better or for worse.

Even the children moved calmly and respectfully. Not hurried. Not silly. They had learned more about the land, each other, and the fact that they had survived. They had made it through what they now called the Long Frost.

Lance and Toddy were nearing their sixth season, but the stress of life had unnaturally aged them. They wanted to help, belong, and be a part of their parents' plans, and they did it happily despite their limits.

Lance gently tugged on the sheep's line to keep them close. Toddy busied herself with breakfast. She handed Kale pieces of fish, which he skewered and then placed over the fire. Her small hands moved with purpose, her eyes shining with pride. She didn't just help—she made a difference.

It was a beautiful day, and none of them wanted to leave. Not yet. The sun warmed the bare rock, bringing them comfort they had missed for many moon cycles. Kara knelt down and touched the stone, whispering words she hadn't spoken in weeks: "Thank you."

They will travel again tomorrow, this time south, toward the sun. Though the mountains were getting lower, snow still clung to the ground, making movement difficult. The way ahead was unclear, but today—today was special.

A low hum rose from the stone, like wind caught in a throat. Sang stepped up, eyes wide. "What is that?"

Chapter 3

Cave of Songs

They stopped; before them was a gaping hole in the mountain face. The trail they were following divided; one set of prints entered the cave, and the other passed by it. Emanating from the cave's dark throat came a low, melodic hum. While the leaders resolved their next step, Toddy took matters into her own hands.

The sound emanating from the cave didn't bother Toddy at all, although it unsettled the others. The almost-adults argued about what to do; apparently, they needed to talk about it.

Toddy felt an inexplicable pull toward the humming sound, as though the cave itself was calling to her. Without waiting for agreement or reassurance, she reached for Lance's hand. Together, they stepped forward, entering the natural cathedral formed by the cavern's towering stone walls, drawn onward by the song that echoed within.

They vanished into the dark before Kara realized they were gone. Drud rushed in after them, fear tightening his chest. He nearly collided with the children just a few steps in. They stood still, looking up at the sparkling ice stalactites that sang as the wind passed through.

The rest of the clan instantly followed. There was room to breathe, but the moment pressed them close. Kara inhaled sharply; she was pulled back to a time before her mother died, when she sang their joyful song. The cave echoed it back, and it sounded strangely familiar. The cave knows.

Kale built a fire at the entrance, the sharp crackle of dry twigs echoing against the stone walls while tendrils of smoke curled into the chilly air. He worked quickly, knowing the fire's warmth and light would help keep wild animals at bay. Drud added thick branches, their rough bark hissing as the flames licked upward, and then waited for them to catch, glancing nervously into the gathering shadows beyond the cave's mouth.

Drud handed out torches. He wanted to know where the cave ended. If there were no bears, then they could stay until the air outside warms.

The cave was vast; it had high, smooth walls, and fresh air flowed through. If the land outside were more forgiving, this cave might be a good place to build a future. But the question remained: was this cave merely shelter or something more?

It was clear that animals had used the path leading here to escape the cold. But the trail felt ritualistic, worn not just for survival but with purpose.

While Kara and Sang began preparing a late meal, Drud and Kale returned to the cave's entrance. Using walking sticks to avoid any chance of falling, they followed the secondary trail west.

The trail was icy and slippery, and the sticks gave them a better chance of avoiding injuries. An accident now would require them to stay in place until they were well enough to continue. That would put a strain on their limited supplies.

They hadn't gone very far before reaching a flat, wide area carved into the mountain's side. It felt like a place to wait. A boundary. Beyond that, the trail had vanished.

After a quiet moment, each observing their surroundings, Kale said, "Maybe it's where you wait until it's your turn."

Drud frowned. "What would they be waiting for?"

Kale had nothing.

Returning to the cave, the aroma of bear meat cooking over an open fire caught their attention. Kale, ever the tinkerer, had built a collapsible spit, so they wouldn't need to gather branches each time one was needed. They could not be happier; torches ringed the fire pit, casting flickering shadows on the cave wall.

Then something odd took place. Drud and Kale saw the flames bend—each torch flame was leaning toward the back of the cave.

Drud placed his slab of bear meat on a rabbit skin. With a torch in hand, he disappeared into the darkness. In just a few steps, the flame weakened as the wind grew stronger, now horizontal to the cave floor, pointing deeper into the tunnel. He lowered his torch to the cave floor. Tracks. Many different kinds of animals had come through here. A side road. But to where?

A few hundred feet inside, the air grew humid. The temperature rose. The warm cave was not just a shelter—it was a passage. He puzzled over how animals navigated the dark without torches.

He returned to the clan and shared what he had seen. Now he understood the trail outside. Animals waited their turn behind a leader who knew the way. But why? What lay beyond?

They slept within the protection of the rock walls. The cave sang softly all around them. Tomorrow they would find out what waited in the dark.

Chapter 4

Forked Flame

Drud gave each child a small torch, not just for light but to make them feel like they belonged. To carry a flame was to have a purpose.

Kale followed, with a braided line tying him to the sheep. Then the wolves came next, quiet and watchful. Sang walked behind them. Kara paused, listening for the cave's breath.

Bing was free to lead. He walked into the darkness armed with nature's gifts—smell, instinct, and listening to the sound of the wind. He wasn't just a scout; he was a signal.

They walked in a line. Drud waited until Bing's footsteps faded, then he raised his torch to the wind and followed. The flame bent slowly, guiding the way. Even with the torches, they could only see a few feet ahead. Drud walked beside the slowest person in the group. They moved carefully, then faster as confidence grew.

Everything was fine—until the path forked. Drud mumbled something that might have been "crap" if such a word existed.

Drud was unsure. The flame bent again, this time to the right. He trusted it.

A vast, quiet cavern opened up before them. They stopped to rest. Sang made a fire—not for warmth, but to cook. The cavern was warm, and their torchlight was dim but not frightening.

Kara, always alert, wondered how far they'd have to go to reach the other side—if there was one. She looked up. What she saw took her breath away.

The smoke from the fire split into two streams, drifting in opposite directions. It wasn't chance. Nature was trying to confuse them.

She tapped Drud's toe. He followed her gaze and saw the split.

"Yes, it's a problem," he said. "But it's also a sign."

Drud relayed his concerns to Sang and Kale. As they spoke in low voices, torchlight cast long, restless shadows on the damp cave walls. Their voices mingled with the distant drip of water.

Drud and Kale took charge while the clan and animals waited in tense silence. Every member—men and women—shared the burden of decisions. Kara watched as the two leaders faded into the darkness.

Kale's path came to an end. A wide pit yawned across the cave floor. He stretched his arm, holding the torch over the chasm. The flame was pulled downward. He tossed a rock. It took a long time for a faint echo to return.

He decided to go back; they could not pass through this way.

Drud's path went on without stopping. After an unknown stretch of time, light appeared—an exit leading to another trail.

It was clear what to do. The fire had chosen.

Chapter 5

Bing's Back

The guide returned. The fog lifted. The stream sang.

A beast jumped out of the dark and into the flickering mist. First came fear—then joy. Bing was back.

He bounded toward Kara and licked her face, his way of showing love. She hugged him, feeling cold in his fur. He had been outside in the frost. He wasn't just their pet; he was part of the clan.

After their reunion, Bing stepped into the shadows, paused, and looked back, as if to say, "Come with me," and then disappeared again. The clan followed.

They had lost track of time; they must have traveled a great distance and still have not found Drud.

They had camped one more night in the cave, or so they assumed. They had no idea if it was night or day. Still no Drud.

The sun was setting when they emerged from the long cave. Mountains, shrouded in mist, rose into a darkening sky. A ribbon of color stretched across the horizon—sky blue fading to yellow, then orange, then black.

Bing disappeared again in the fading light, but his loud run through the trees gave him away. Drud smiled when he heard his wolf chasing down the mountain. There was no snow now, and the trees surrounded him. He was below the snow line.

Faces filled with relief greeted Drud and Bing when they returned to the cave. The sounds of joy gave way to the murmur of a stream below—water that hadn't frozen. A very good sign.

They zigzagged through the trees and arrived at an open space. Bing stood in the center. He appeared tired, but not too tired to prevent him from doing a happy dance with his brothers and sisters.

Kara's brow furrowed in surprise. Bing had found them the perfect place to camp, a flat piece of land beside a stream that flowed gently over a natural rock weir. The water fell into a calm pool, then flowed through a channel full of rocks and out of sight, disappearing into the trees.

Kale got to the stream first and smiled. He pointed to the calm waters below the falls.

"That's where the big fish wait," he said. They gather below waterfalls because the current makes a basin for them to rest in, and anything small is swept over and eaten."

Pleased with his lecture, he grabbed his gear and was gone.

Kara insisted that they set up the hut even though the weather was perfect. The clan went about their tasks with the ease of a seasoned troop. When Kale returned with a string of fish, the camp had been set up and was ready for their meal to be prepared.

Everyone waited patiently while the master cook and fisherman made their late meal. Kara and Sang sat quietly, petting the wolves curled up in the furs next to them.

The days in the cave had left them quiet.

They said little. With full bellies, they lay down on their pallets and drifted away.

Kara whispered a name for the place, "Bing's Crossing," before she closed her eyes.

Toddy, who was half asleep, said it again and again like a prayer. The stream kept singing.

Chapter 6

Kara's Vision: The Line of Mothers

Kara drifted in a space between sleep and memory. A line of women—old, weathered, and beautiful—stretched before her. They held hands across centuries, each one whispering to the next.

The first mother said in a language older than fire, "I hid the names of the hunted in my breath. I learned what silence looks like—and how to use it."

The second mother said, "I sewed warnings into lullabies. I taught my girls to smile with their mouths closed."

The third mother said. "I buried a map under the hearthstone. She will know where to dig when the time comes."

Each mother taught her children how to survive. Some fought. Some watched. Some made things. But each carried a secret—powerful, quiet, and sacred.

Kara heard the whispers merge into one voice: "We do not forget. We do not speak until the time is right. Our secrets are not shameful; they're part of the plan. We are not giving up when we are quiet—we are planting seeds. They will know when the daughters rise. They will use what we have saved."

Kara felt Toddy's name stir in her chest. Now she knew: her job was to prepare and open her up to both the old and new worlds. Her task was to pass on the memories, which was hidden in ritual, and to wait for the right individuals to unlock it.

She woke with a new level of clarity. Yes, she needs to provide this wisdom to Toddy when the time is right. But a new thought flooded her, like a ripple from the vision.

Is there going to be another girl?

She looked to her right, questioning Drud?

The question was not pointless; it was ancestral. The question was steeped in history, tradition, and mythology. These events changed everything. It wasn't just about survival in a new land; it was sacred. She would need to create a deliberate space—a sacred distance. Not to sever ties with other clans, but to ensure that any future union would be chosen with ritual, memory, and mythic intent.

Isolation would not protect the purity of her line. Stories would. Truths would. They paid tribute to those they held dear. They conveyed the message to those they respected.

Blood alone would not complete the circle. Only those who heard the land, the silence between songs, and the old mothers' whispers would shape it.

If Kale and Sang could remember the past, they might still belong. Kara would not decide lightly. Her life was no longer just living. It was a legacy.

And her gut told her: only the mothers' chosen would lead the rightful heirs into their fold.

The answer made her happy.

Chapter 7

Echoes of Someone's Past

The screech of an alpine lynx and the panicked bleating of sheep jolted Kara awake. Drud was already outside; Kara and Kale were right behind him. As was custom, Sang gathered the flock and led them inside.

It was too late. One bundle of food was missing. Five wolves were chasing the lynx—small and unnaturally strong—up the mountain.

It was a small loss. The stolen bundle might have fed them for a few days, but they would survive. The loss of even one wolf would hurt them more. They had come to depend on them for protection, company, and as a warning system. This time, though, the wolves had failed. It would have been remarkable to see the cat jump from ledge to ledge, clutching its prize in its mouth. In better times, such a sight might have been something to behold. But now there is a thief to hunt.

The wolves, heavier and more eager, chased without thought. No one could say who led the charge. They were too deep in the woods. The chase brought them to a snow-covered ledge. One wolf, trying to cut off the lynx, leaped into a snowdrift and triggered a disaster.

A piece of cornice broke off. The wolf was devoured by the moving mass.

Kale had seen what an avalanche cascading down the slopes could do. Without hesitation, he led everyone back to the hut, sheltered by a protective brow.

It began quietly. Then came the roar, like thunder, as tons of snow fell. The hut shook. Minutes passed.

Then they waited.

Drud was the first to leave. He ran to the last place they stood and scanned the slope.

The mountain was covered in a mist of light snow. Then it all settled gently to the ground.

There were no wolves to be seen, just an eerie emptiness. He felt a loss like that of a severed limb.

Kale, Kara, and Drud dug through the snow for hours, salvaging what they could. The root vegetables had been kept inside. They had buried the dried fish and meat in a snowbank; that was not a problem.

By day's end, they had rebuilt enough of the travois to put the sheep to work. Then they paused and waited, hoping the wolves if any had survived, would return.

They were thankful for Kale's past experiences. He had seen avalanches before. He didn't care about the praise. "It's what anyone would have done." He said.

They had planned to descend to lower ground the next day. Now they would stay. Not out of fear, but loyalty. They wouldn't leave until they knew what had happened to their wolves.

They still hadn't found the right words to say how worried they were. Their concerns were not limited to the wolves but also extended to the safety of the new clan.

Chapter 8

Day Three

They couldn't wait any longer. The cold was ending, and the snowmelt would soon begin—threatening to wash them off the mountain. It was time.

While waiting, Kale spent his spare time crafting a map on bobcat skin. From a ledge above the trees, he could see all the way to the sea, many moons away.

In the morning light, he saw two columns of smoke rising from the lower peaks. He marked a charcoal path to avoid those camps, as he'd done before. By nightfall, the smoke vanished—replaced by an orange glow. One fire burned brighter than the rest, lighting up the hills. That camp was large, possibly dangerous.

On the third day, they began their descent. Kale led the way. The group walked in a straight line. Kara walked with the children; two of the lambs echoed their steps. Sang led the rest of the flock. Drud came last, eyes scanning the trail for the wolves, as always.

Drud was still amazed at how quiet a marauder could be. He was struck from behind. Instinctively, he pulled out his knife, then a wet, sloppy tongue washed his face. He didn't know who was happier, him or the wolf.

The rest of the furry family followed, bounding toward the children and joyful adults. Kale remained on guard, always alert. He would have time later to run his hands through their thick coats.

Toddy was the first to notice. She turned back up the trail, her eyes going blank. She asked in a small voice, “Where is he?”

Bing was missing.

The play ended. Joy gave way to worry. They had to wait.

The camp was ready. The fire was started. But the warmth was empty.

Where was he?

Chapter 9

They Are Coming

Kale couldn't see them, but he could hear them.

No doubt about it: loud, careless people. A small group like theirs moved quietly. But this pack moved without care. That meant numbers. That meant being sure of themselves. That meant trouble.

They felt safe here. They moved around without caution because they believed they owned this land.

Kale hurried back to camp. He warned the others. They would have to leave. That choice meant Bing would be lost.

Kale carefully guided the group around the advancing clan, steering them into a narrow split between the mountains. His confidence came from experience; he believed that a run-off river would eventually lead them to the sea.

Keeping the group's safety in mind, he led them along a path above the wash line—a clear mark left behind by previous floods.

The wash line was formed by the force of rushing water during the snowmelt, and no one could predict when the next surge might come barreling down the ravine. By traveling above this line, Kale ensured that the group would stay out of danger, safe from sudden floods, and dry for the journey ahead.

The wolves moved freely; they would not be burdened by towing travois, as they needed to be unencumbered to protect the clan. Drud was particularly impressed with the wealth of materials strewn about the landscape. Everything they would need to fabricate shelters and weapons.

Toddy and Lance kept glancing back up the path, always hoping to see Bing.

By midday, the noise of the clan moving forward had faded. Kale, seasoned and alert, told the group to stop. He spoke to Drud in a low voice. Then they vanished into the thick woods, spears in hand. Kara and Sang accepted the fact that starting a fire now was too dangerous. So they prepared a cold meal.

Kale liked the sound of running water. He had only walked a few hundred steps when he heard the familiar rush. The rougher the water, the bigger the fish, waiting with their mouths open beneath the falls.

He was right.

He waded into the cold, nearly still water beneath the falls, spear in hand. He didn't move. The fish would come to him.

A deep pool had formed under the falling water. Fish swam in the churning current, hoping for food from above. They drifted into the calm waters to rest, mouths full, and that was where Kale waited.

He came back an hour later with seven large trout.

The hut was built, but there was no fire. He pointed at the shelter. “Light a fire in there,” he said. “It will hide the flame.” They were eating fresh trout less than an hour later. Life was good again, but a hint of sadness lingered.

The following morning, the group descended further into a forest of oak and walnut trees, trees untouched by people.

A new land to explore. A promising new adventure lay ahead. There could also be new threats to deal with.

Chapter 10

The One Beneath the Snow

Bing didn't panic.

Snow pressed in from all sides, making everything quiet and white. But Bing wasn't made to panic. He was made to persist.

His lungs slowly drew in life-giving air from a shrinking pocket in the snow. His paws are digging at the snow, not frantically but with purpose. He dug toward the lightest snow, where the cold felt less thick. He didn't know why, but he knew it was right.

With each push, the snow behind him packed tight, sealing off the tunnel. Bing didn't stop, though. He dug steadily, like a mole sniffing out a tasty grub. He fought on, steady and strong with unwavering determination.

There was no fear. No doubt. Just movement.

The snow became powder.

Then brightened. Then he saw the sky.

He burst from the drift with an explosion of snow, tail thrashing the wispy drift behind him. He didn't stop. He sniffed the air, turned to the forest below, and ran.

The scent trail was weak but familiar. His group was far ahead. Time didn't matter. Distance didn't matter. The trail was everything.

But he wasn't alone.

Two days after the clan had moved on, Bing had become prey. A hungry snow leopard had picked up his scent. The cat was nearly his size and desperate. Cold drains energy faster than hunger. The leopard needed meat.

Bing heard the soft pads crushing the snow behind him. He turned away from the cliffs and into the woods, where his nose and ears gave him an edge. He wasn't a sheep. He would not die easily.

The cat followed.

Bing veered toward a bluff that he should have avoided. He ran toward salvation, up a steep hill, and positioned himself on a ledge fifteen feet above the trail. He crouched, silent.

The leopard moved slowly and carefully. It sniffed at the air. Bing's scent was strong. The cat tensed.

There was not enough time to evade his prey.

Bing leaped from the ledge with the swiftness of a meteor, his jaws firmly gripping the cat's neck. They rolled, tangled in the snow, and both were frantic. Bing held on as the cat twisted.

In their struggle, they rolled over a broken sapling jutting out of the snow. As if waiting for this moment.

With one last roll, Bing's jaws still gripping the cat's neck, the violent motion left the cat impaled on the tree. Bing didn't move. He remained still, silent, his breath calmed. Then he let go.

A wolf would only eat a cat if it were starving. Bing was very hungry.

With his stomach full, he ran. The trail was fading. But the pack was in front. He would look for them.

He would find them.

Chapter 11

The Plateau That Broke

They had made it to high ground.

The clan laughed, and it wasn't a fake laugh. The plateau was wide, sunlit, and quiet. For the first time in a long while, they felt safe.

Drud saw Toddy walking near the edge. He opened his mouth to call her back.

Then the earth began to shudder.

A low rumble. Then a crack. The plateau fractured like ice and tilted toward the valley below.

Toddy turned around. She locked eyes with Drud. Then she began to slide.

Drud ran to her as the ground gave way beneath him. He clawed forward, his lungs burning with panic.

He wouldn't reach her in time.

Then, Bing burst onto the slope, bounding across the crumbling ground. He bit down on Toddy's tunic and backed up the sliding ground, using four paws to gain footing where two feet could not.

Drud struggled. The cliff collapsed. He fell.

A rope caught him—Kara's safety line draped over his shoulders. He reached for it, and with a single hand, he swung, suspended breathlessly in the still air.

Bing reached the ledge above. Toddy was safe.

Drud climbed, inch by inch, and Kara and Kale pulled him up to solid ground.

He collapsed, exhausted. Bing licked his face over and over again, happily; it was just another day in the life of a wolf.

Kara held Toddy tightly in her arms. Tears streamed down her cheeks; her little girl was alive.

They didn't start a fire that night. They sat quietly, not because there was any concern for their safety; it was because the darkness was soothing.

Kara spoke. She held the rope up to the stars and recited words passed down to her through a line of mothers: "Nature works against us every day, but it also gives us what we need; we must thank the dangerous earth for the good it gives."

She cut the rope shorter and tied it around Bing's neck.

"This token will make sure your bravery never wavers."

The next day, the sky was clear. Kale and Drud studied the map. Kale said, "We should go toward the sun. But..."

"But what?"

"If other clans came before us, they'd take the easy way. That means we must not follow the easy path."

Drud nodded. "Then we go the hard way. To stay away from other people."

He didn't wait for an answer.

Chapter 12

The Fever That Speaks

By midday, they reached the bottom of the plateau. Debris from past ice slides littered the ground.

They found Cro-Magnon and Neanderthal bones in the loose dirt. Not scattered. Not broken. Aligned.

Like killings had taken place.

Drud looked at Kale. No words were needed.

Out of caution and the fear of running afoul of any dangerous clan, they wouldn't go down into the valley below them.

With head held high, Bing trotted westward. They were all amazed at how he knew to lead them away from danger.

They followed.

It wasn't just a path. It was a fact. Sometimes, pure instinct is wiser than fear. The people left on earth were tough—shaped by necessity, tempered by survival. What Kara was seeing was rare. She could see that Sang was beginning to weaken. Like a shadow, worry grew.

An injured soldier needs help from others in any unit. But here, there were no others. Sang's condition was deteriorating, and the journey needed to stop, and soon.

Kara waited until they were out of earshot at the next break. She whispered her concerns to Drud.

He responded immediately, "We may have to set up a semi-permanent camp here."

After their chores were completed, Drud called the clan together for a planning circle.

There was no reason to leave Sang out. First, Drud turned to her. "Do you know what's wrong with you?"

Sang pulled back her legging. The wound was small but inflamed.

It was a scrape she had gotten when she bumped against the cave wall. She hadn't told anyone. She hadn't slowed down. But now, a week later, it was disabling her.

Kara crouched down beside her, worry etched on her face. She had learned to heal, but what she was looking at was new. She removed a small amount of bitter root from her leather pouch. When nothing else works, start with the obvious.

She could see that Sang was suffering. Red lines climbed toward her hip. Her skin was pale. Her breath was shallow. The fever knew her name.

Toddy knelt beside her. She placed her small hands on Sang's shoulder, wishing that it might soothe her. Kara wrung out rabbit fur that had been soaked in bitter root. She spoke softly, with confidence. "She's on fire."

Lance sat nearby, a knife across his lap, watching the valley below like a guard.

Kara said, "If the fever speaks by moonrise, we answer. We give our voice if it needs it."

She drew a circle of ash around Sang's body. "We call the disease out. We call it. We name it. We shame it. We bind it to the stone."

Kara placed a carved wolf tooth at Sang's feet. Toddy laid down a leaf and branch. Lance put his blade next to Sang's hand. "If she wakes up, she'll know she belongs," he said.

The ceremony continued.

Kara said the names of people who had survived serious sickness before. Sang whispered stories of warmth, family, and the ember that never dies. Lance kept an eye on things.

Sang woke by dawn. Her eyes opened, unfocused. The fever had not sounded its call loudly enough to claim her; she was grateful to be alive. The others woke to the smell of mountain hare roasting over the fire, which mixed with the cool dawn and the soft crackle of burning wood.

Kale and Drud had left camp in the morning to hunt fresh meat. They would stay as long as needed.

When all were fed and their leaders returned, they would leave. Sang felt no fellowship with this place. It had tried to kill her.

Chapter 13

The Valley of Signs

The mountains rose in the distance, different now. They no longer seem frightening. The ground softened and turned green, and the air warmed. Trees grew wider, and the breeze carried the scent of water.

They had entered a quiet valley. Sang walked without pain. Her leg, once a burden, now bore the scar of survival. Kara carved a spiral with three points into her walking stick. It meant "come back."

The wolves would come and go without any form of restraint. Bing stayed close to Toddy, like a sentinel. She sang a song she claimed came from the cave walls. Lance took an interest in the birds circling overhead. "If they sing, it means that we are safe."

Then a sign, "People." A ring of stones that is too perfect to be natural. A tree with bark that has been peeled in a spiral. A fire pit cold, but new.

Keeping with established practice, contact was not possible. The risk was the same for both Neanderthals and Cro-Magnons. Fear turned men into monsters. And there was no room for monsters in the clan.

Kara said nothing, but her eyes lingered on the fire pit. She knew that someday, survival would require unity. But not today. Today's worry was quieter, stranger.

The structure they discovered was not a hut. Not a cave. A dome of branches, covered in moss and feathers. Inside lay a circle of stones, which was a symbol: a handprint pressed into the clay, hardened by fire.

No one spoke.

Toddy reached out and then stopped. "It's not ours."

Drud nodded. "It does not appear to be a warning of any kind." Kale knelt beside it. "It could be a message. Or a sign. Or a memory."

They made camp nearby, but not too close. That night Kara dreamed of a woman with feathers in her hair, who sang to a fire that never went out.

She woke up from her dream and said one word: "Before."

Chapter 14

The Answer in the Ash

The valley held its breath.

Morning came slowly, with mist and birdsong. Kara, as always, rose before the others. Her dream clung to her skin like smoke.

The woman with feathers hadn't spoken, but her silence meant something. She sang to an eternal fire that never extinguished and pressed her hand into clay as if to say, "Remember me."

Kara walked to the dome. The handprint remained within the circle of stones, untouched. She crouched beside it, letting the cool air brush her skin and listening to the faint rustle of leaves beyond the dome. Her fingers hovered just above the stone, but she didn't disturb it—a quiet patience settled around her. Kara's breath slowed as she focused on every subtle sound, her gaze tracing the handprint's edges.

She resisted the urge to reach out, choosing instead to observe, to listen, and to let the silence speak. In that stillness, her curiosity deepened, and she wondered what story the mark held, what memory lingered here, waiting for her to understand.

Toddy silently approached her and asked. "The mother, she was real, wasn't she?

Kara nodded. "She is not, but she shall be."

Toddy didn't ask what that meant. She just sat next to her mother and placed her hand on the ground.

Lance joined them, scanning the hills. He said, "We're not alone. But they aren't coming."

Kara returned to the riverbank and scraped up a handful of clay. She didn't explain why. She didn't have to.

The clan watched as she shaped a flat disc, pressed her hand into it, and then gave it to Toddy and Lance.

They each left their mark. Kara carved a spiral in the center, the same symbol on Sang's walking stick.

Drud put the disk in the fire. Bing let out a soft howl, as if to bless it.

They buried the hardened clay under a pile of feathers and moss. No words were spoken.

That night, Kara said. "This valley is not our home; it is a memory. Someone lived here. Someone sang a song to this earth. Someone is telling us to be careful."

She turned to her clan and spoke to them. "We stay alive by moving forward. We get through by remembering."

Lance nodded.

The words hung in the air, reminiscent of a promise.

Chapter 15

The Clan of the Shore

Before the land changed, the wind had become salty and steady, brushing Kara's cheek like a whisper from something vast and old. Trees grew sparse. The ground turned sandy. The wolves were getting restless.

They were close to the sea.

Lance saw smoke rising above a bluff that protected a sheltered inlet. Kara raised her hand, warning them to be cautious. But Bing's body language was calm, as if he were sure of no threat. He loped off to the bluff, looking back as if he were asking permission.

They approached Bing slowly, with their weapons sheathed, and the wolves waited. They took a moment to observe a family of blended men and women camped near the water's edge.

They moved away from the bluff and worked their way down the hill that transformed into a sandy dune. Their noisy approach drew the attention of the people. The small clan did not show any signs of fear as they approached the group. The tenseness that formed in Kara's chest had calmed.

Before them stood a clan, sun-darkened and quiet; they didn't seem to be a threat. Kara smiled at

Bing's assessment of them prior to their meeting. They wore jewelry made from woven reeds and fish bones. A woman who identified herself as Asha, their leader, welcomed them by placing her hand over her heart.

"Our scouts have been observing you for some time," she said. "We were hoping you would come."

Sitting on benches of logs brought from a distant forest, Asha began to tell them the stories of their past. "For many generations, our people had lived near the sea. We were never warriors; we were watchers. Over time we came to know the tides, the best places to fish, and the treachery of salt and wind."

They dug homes into the bluff to withstand the storms. Reed curtains hung over the openings. Shells marked the graves of people who had died in the waves. They shared food: grilled fish, seaweed broth, and flatbread that had been baked on hot stones.

The bread was something new; these clansmen have much to teach them.

Toddy looked about the encampment and noticed that there were no elders. Only grown-ups and children. She whispered her concern to her mother.

Pleased with the young child's keen observation, Kara asked Asha, "Where are your ancestors?"

Asha turned her head toward the sea. "They went in the direction of the setting sun. To look for a better beach. They never came back."

That night, Asha's people shared what they knew. Their knowledge was practical, hard-earned, and exact.

Asha blended warnings with stories: "The sea pulls like sadness. You must float, not fight. Boil dirty water. Filter it. Trade inland. There are others who may offer assistance, but be cautious."

She added, "Cover your eyes with cloth. Cooking with charcoal is better. Make sure your feet are dry. Salt can help in healing, but not always. Travel early or late, never midday. Make sleds out of driftwood and bones to carry your gear. Use stone stacks to mark the tides.

Never camp near the mouth of a river; flash floods come without warning. If birds fly in circles, a storm is coming. If they fly inland, it's already here."

Kara memorized every word.

Others taught Kale how to fish in the big sea. She knew he needed to understand its dangers.

Kale was drawn to the ocean. Even though its vastness frightened him, its rhythm calmed something deep inside. Asha asked him to locate her brother Tovin. "You will find him by the river."

"He will teach you how to read the water: green for shallow areas and silver for schools of fish.

Tovin taught him how to make weighted nets from sinew and stone, showing how these sturdy materials help the nets sink and hold fast in the current. Kale learned to use tidal pools as clever traps, taking advantage of the ebbing water to catch fish more easily. Crafting fishhooks from bone that wouldn't break became a vital skill, with each notch and curve shaped for strength and reliability. He also learned how to cure fish with sun and salt, preserving them for long journeys ahead. Each method connected to the next, forming a tapestry of survival by the sea—every detail rooted in the landscape and tradition.

Contemplating what he had learned, Kale set about sketching new maps. His hand guided by recent memory, he traced charcoal smudges of shifting tides and secret places where fish gathered. He included safe havens where the wind softened and the salt air gently blew.

The cool breeze tugged at his hair, carrying whispers of distant storms and the tang of brine—each sensation a silent guide. He asked about the blue sea, even though no one called it that aloud.

Tovin, his mentor and the village's navigator, replied, his voice steady and distant like the horizon, "There is a sea beyond the broken one. It is blue like memory and harsh like time." His words poured across the sand, shaping the silence between them.

Kale marked it anyway: "blue sea." The name shimmered on the page, as if naming it could tame its vastness or restore something lost to the wind and waves.

Asha turned their attention to the shore. A long-held warning about their savior, the great waters to the south, she said. "The sea is beautiful. But it doesn't love you."

Her lessons continued. “Remain vigilant,” she went on to instruct them on how to identify rip currents, water that moves faster than the waves around them. How to float on their backs if they get pulled out to sea. To use stones and shells to mark safe paths.

She taught them to use dried seaweed and fish oil to make signal fires. “Listen to the wind,” she explained. “The change is its warning to you.”

“Has anyone ever been taken?” Toddy asked. Asha nodded.

“Yes. But it will not take you, if you remember.”

“What is beyond the Broken Delta?” Lance asked.

Asha paused. “We think there are cliffs. A place where the water warms. But we don’t go there. The land loses its shape.”

Just before they left, Bing unearthed a carved stone near the bluff. It bore a spiral Kara recognized from old maps.

Asha said, “Some who reach the delta never come back. Some people return...different. They speak of voices in the mist. Of totems made of bones.”

“Do you believe them?” Kara asked.

“I think the sea is older than truth,” Asha said. “and it doesn’t care what we believe.”

Chapter 16

Crossing the Broken Delta

They stayed thirteen days with the Shore Clan, long enough to glean critical lessons for surviving the sea's threats.

With a bone blade, Toddy learned how to gut fish and read the wind's warnings. Lance learned how to read the tides' moods and shape driftwood into spears. Asha taught them how to survive and how to remember.

The Shore Clan gave them knowledge, strength, peace, and a quiet exchange of skill and ritual.

On the morning of the fourteenth day, Kara stood at the edge of the delta. "We cross today," she said. "Not because we are ready. We must discover our place in thc world."

The Broken Delta lay before them, fractured into many rivers, sandbars, and marshland. It was a place where the land lost its shape and the water lost its name.

The rafts they built had flat bottoms and wide beams and could be pulled across the shifting water.

The Shore Clan gave them the animal hides, driftwood, and sinew lashings. Each raft bore a special mark. Kara's raft was marked with a spiral flame, a feather, and a stone that represented Toddy. Lance's raft was marked with three notches—one for each river they'd crossed.

Before they left, Kara led a ceremony.

Performing what has become a special custom, each person pressed their hand into clay, marked it with ash, and placed it in a circle around the fire.

Asha placed hers last. "We won't walk with you." She said. "But we will think of you."

They departed at sunrise.

The delta was quiet. Water twisted through the land like veins. Channels broke apart and reformed. Sandbars shifted. The air smelled of salt, rot, and something older.

They moved slowly, pulling the rafts over gravel tongues and mudflats. Bing and the wolves walked ahead. Kale guarded the maps. Lance watched the sky. Toddy left feathers and stones along the path.

On the second day, fog rolled in. It came in from the sea—thick, wet, and quiet. Visibility dropped to a few feet. The sound was muffled. The wolves grew nervous.

Kara asked them to be silent.

They tied the rafts together with ropes. Between Bing and Kyler, Toddy and Lance were placed for safety. The sheep followed; there was no need to tether them anymore. They were members of the clan. They pulled the rafts by hand to the shore's edge.

Then there was the sound.

A splash. A hiss. Something moved in the water. Kale saw a flash of something beneath the surface and shouted a warning to Drud and Kara. "Teeth." Drud raised his spear. Kara lit a torch. The fog glowed orange. Shapes moved beneath the surface—long, wavy, and hungry. They didn't approach, but they did follow. Kara taught them as they walked, her voice steady: "Float. Don't thrash. Don't scream if you are bitten. Fight back. If you lose your way, listen for the wolves. They always find their way back."

Toddy repeated the rules out loud. Lance whispered them.

As the sun was setting, the fog began to fade. They reached a wide, dry sandbar and rested. No one spoke of the shapes in the water. That night, Kara started a new ritual.

She placed a spiral stone in the center of camp. "This is not our land. But the present is our trial. We mark it not to claim it, but to remember it." Each one gave the river their chosen token.

The land rose before them in a vista of green and rolling hills, and their shadows cast long omens of what was to come.

The blue sea was patient. Kara turned back toward the delta.

"It tried to erase us," she said. "But we won't forget."

Chapter 17

The Teeth Beneath

The land to the west of the delta wasn't land; it was memory pretending to be solid.

Mudflats became marshes thick with reeds. Water clung to their ankles like something alive. The wolves moved carefully. Bing growled at things unseen. Even the wind seemed unsure.

They moved quietly, pulling the rafts over slippery ground, stopping only to inspect the children's footwear and tighten lashings. Kara walked with her spear raised, signaling she would strike first if need be.

Toddy carried her bag of feathers—feathers she had been collecting since their confrontation with the Valley People. She also kept a few stones that were important to her. Lance carried his blade.

The children were small, but they were no longer soft. The Shore Clan had taught them how to read the tides and clean fish.

But this place needed a much older spirit to guide them. Toddy would ask her mother to speak with the line of mothers.

The marsh narrowed into a channel flanked by tall reeds. Bing stopped. His ears flattened. The wolves circled the children, forming a protective barrier.

Then, a long, scaled body emerged from the dark water. Teeth gnashed. Eyes were void of life. It struck Drud, knocking him back. Sang screamed. Kara did not.

Sang moved like she had done it before; her spear hit the creature's jaw, but it twisted and wrapped around the spear shaft. Lance didn't hesitate. He lunged, blade in hand, and stabbed it in the eye.

It thrashed. Mud and blood churned. The wolves leaped. Toddy pulled Lance back just before the tail whipped past.

Then, silence.

The creature's school vanished. The water stilled. Drud's leg was injured. Kara applied ash paste and wrapped it in soft rabbit fur. Kale remained alert and silent. Lance sat beside the dead barracuda, staring at the blade still lodged in its head.

Kara knelt beside him and placed her hand on his head. "You didn't think twice," she said.

Lance replied, "I didn't think; I remembered."

Toddy put a feather on the creature's head. "It was hungry," she said in a low voice. "But we were hungrier."

That night, they built a fire to celebrate their good fortune. Kara led a ritual, not as a boast but as a warning to stay alert.

She made the shape of the creature in ash. "This is a symbol of what waits for us," she said. "Destiny doesn't chase us. It doesn't warn. It strikes."

Every member left a mark. Kale a spiral to confuse. Drud drew a jagged line to the wound. Toddy, a circle for the time before. Lance, a slash for the time after.

Kara put in a flame. "This is how we remember," she said. "Don't be afraid, teach.

The stars came out late, reluctant. The wolves curled around the children. Kara sat with her spear across her knees, watching the water.

Lance slept with his precious knife beside him. Toddy told the fire stories of teeth, feathers, and the moment before.

The marsh was still. But they weren't.

They had learned.

The sheep were oblivious to the dangers surrounding them.

Chapter 18

The Signal Fire

Toddy carried her bag of stones and feathers. Lance had his knife. Kara was quiet, and relief softened her face.

They had made it across the delta. They had faced the harsh truth. The wind shifted.

It came from the south, sharp and dry. The sky darkened, not with clouds, but with memory. Kara felt it in her ribs. It was a storm that not only toppled trees but also shattered stories.

She said nothing, fearing words would give it life.

At midday, the wind had teeth.

It tore at the rafts, blew sand into their eyes, and howled over the ground. Bing howled once and then stopped. The wolves made a dash for the ridge.

Kale tightened the bindings holding the rafts in place. Drud swore at the sky. Kara didn't move.

She remembered this wind, not from this place, but from the stories her mother had told. This wind was referred to as the wind from the sea.

The wind from the sea was the story that preceded her memory loss.

She knelt and put her hand on the ground. It was hot. Too hot. “We stop here,” she said.

They set up a low camp behind a rock outcrop. No fire. No talking. Just preparation for the mystery to unravel.

Toddy sat alone, arranging her feathers in a spiral. Lance busied himself knapping a keen edge on his knife. Kara watched them both.

Sang stood up as the wind rose.

She walked to the center of camp and made a triangle with a feather, a stone, and a piece of bone. She then lit a single flame.

She hadn’t been told to.

Kara rose slowly, approached, not sure of her ritual, and knelt and asked. “What is this?”

Sang didn’t look up. “A signal.”

“To whom?” Kara asked.

“To those who remember.” She replied

Kara nodded. “Then let it burn.”

The flame held. The wind howled. But the triangle didn’t break.

The sky turned dark, a wide crimson line bleeding across the horizon. The wolves howled. The wind lifted and dropped the rafts. Drud was slammed against a stone outcropping. Kale used his body to protect the children.

Kara stood in defiance, her arms outstretched, keeping her eyes closed.

She whispered names, not of the living, but of her ancestors. Names not spoken since the last crossing. She uttered these names with fierce determination.

The wind didn't stop. But it bent.

By nightfall, the storm had passed. The camp was scattered but alive. The fire still burned. Sang sat next to it, unmoving, eyes open.

They rebuilt the camp without saying a word. Kara tended to Drud's bruises. Kale retied the rafts. Lance sat next to Toddy and watched the fire.

"You didn't run," he said. Toddy shook her head. "It wasn't chasing."

Kara approached. She placed a new feather in the triangle. "This is how storms are remembered. Not by what they take. But by what they don't."

Toddy put in a stone. Lance put in a new token: the tooth of a barracuda, making the triangle a square.

The stars returned.

The wolves lay at camp's edge. Kara sat with her back to the wind, eyes on the fire. Toddy whispered to the flames; Lance stood guard.

One wolf watched, his eyes focused on the fire.

Chapter 19

The Clan of Echoes

The land rose in slow, careful folds, as if the earth itself were preparing for something. Wind-worn and sparse, scrub brush clung to the hillsides. The stones underfoot still remembered the frost.

The clan hoped for warmth here, sunshine, salt air, and the chance to rest. But the Blue Sea wasn't in their stories yet. It was colder. Wilder. Uneasy.

Kara walked with her spear raised, ever on alert, casting her eyes to the horizon, looking for warnings.

The wind brought a smell of distant snow. The sky changed its mind without asking. The sky was clear one moment and cloudy the next.

The elders had spoken of places like these. This is where the sun's promise has been broken. Where the sea rose not with waves, but with hunger.

Kale said it first. "This isn't spring." Kara nodded. "It's the edge of something colder."

They kept going.

The sheep had gone quiet.

Their hooves made a soft sound on stone. The wind guided them. Kara was concerned when they were wending their way through the marsh, but now she noticed that they moved with purpose.

Five of the seven sheep survived the journey.

Brindle, the matriarch, nudged Toddy when she wandered too far; the ground was patchy and uneven. Moss, who was small and round, followed Lance like a broken reed. Thorn, thin and restless, ears twitching at every sound. Echo, born during the crossing, was pale and quiet, her bleat soft and eerie. Rook, black-faced and very stubborn, once charged Bing and lived. He walked wherever he pleased. They were more than food. They were more than just wool. Their rhythm was akin to that of the wolves. Even so, someday, they may be their means of survival.

On the third day, they came upon the clan of Echos.

First there was a ring of stones, and a fire burned. They stood back. No weapons drawn.

The people were quiet and older than expected. Nema, their leader, wore a cloak made of woven bark. She spoke like wind through reeds. "We saw your signal." She said. "We understood your spiral."

Kara stepped forward. "We crossed the delta. We faced the teeth it shared with water and set the wind free."

Nema understood. "Now you are ready to listen."

They spent three nights with the elderly clan. Kara wondered whether or not they were the ones who once left Asha's shores.

The Clan of Echoes offered them shelter. They recounted tales of the sea and of terrible storms.

“It’s not the sky that makes it cold,” Nema said. “It’s the land itself. There is a season when the sun forgets. When the wind returns. When the sea rises with ill intent.”

Kara listened. Toddy watched the two women express their shared reality. She was learning.

Chapter 20

The Trial of the Salt Wind

On the second morning, the wind changed.

It came from the sea, not warm or gentle, but sharp and salty, like a knife dipped in brine. It scraped the skin and whispered to their bones. The clan had changed their rhythm, and the land no longer wanted them. It challenged them to their limits.

Kara first felt it in her joints. A stiffness. A warning.

Toddy worried that Echo wouldn't move; she wasn't always aware of her surroundings. Moss lay down and wouldn't rise. Rook, stubborn and wild, stood still as if listening to something beneath the ground.

The salt wind brought more than just bad weather. It brought caution.

They camped near a broken ridge, where stones formed a half-circle, like an old altar. From there, they could see the sea. It was low and wide, and its shoreline stretched farther than they'd imagined. But it didn't shine. It was anger.

That night, it was Kale that fell ill.

His breathing grew shallow. His skin flushed red with fever. He mumbled in his sleep, reaching for things that weren't there. Kara sat beside him, hand on his chest, counting the rise and fall. It wasn't even like the wind.

"He's dreaming," Toddy whispered. "Of what?" She wondered.

"Of the sea," Kara said.

The clan gathered in silence.

They didn't know the sickness's name, but they knew its shape. The wind from the salt sea had brought it. It came when the land turned inward. Nema had warned them to be careful, but warnings weren't enough.

Lance kept watch. He sharpened his knife while keeping his eyes on Kale. He said, "We burn the ridge if he doesn't wake up."

Kara looked at him. "Why?"

"To send the dream back."

That night, Kara dreamed of warnings, a gift from her mother.

She stood on the shore, but the sea had vanished. In its place lay a field of bones—sheep bones and human bones—where spirals, feathers, and names she hadn't spoken yet had been carved.

Her mother stood beside her, wrapped in cloth stained with salt. She said, "You brought them here."

"I thought it would be safe."

"The world is never safe. It only exists to challenge you."

Kara woke up with a salty taste in her mouth.

At dawn, Echo let out a sharp, clear bleat. Kale stirred. He opened his eyes. He didn't speak, but he saw Kara, Toddy, and then Lance.

Toddy placed feathers around Moss, who hadn't moved. She whispered something Kara couldn't hear. Lance stood beside Rook, one hand on the sheep's thick neck, the other on his knife.

They were no longer children. They were heirs.

Kara got up and walked to the ridge that kept watch over the shore.

She placed a stone onto the sand. A symbolic thank you.

She returned to the clan. "We're leaving as soon as we have the sleds readied," she said. "We follow the salt sea. We don't fear it. We name it."

Toddy stepped up. "What should we call it?"

Kara stared at the sea. "The hunger."

They moved on as the sun descended, shadows growing long and quiet. The wind didn't stop. It pushed against them and whispered through the sawgrass. But the clan did not give up.

Brindle followed Toddy. They carried Echo. Thorn walked ahead, his ears twitching. Moss stayed close to Kara. Rook followed no one; he went where he pleased.

The sea waited.

Kara led them into the setting sun. The sea was below them as they marched atop a sand ridge.

Chapter 21

The Salt Clan

Despite the encroaching darkness, they remained unhurried. The coast ran on forever, disappearing along with the horizon. The sight of it was both exhilarating and wonderful.

The sea was wide and low. Its shoreline looked like a wound. Wind had carved the land into terraces and hollows. Salt coated their mouths and collected in the sheep's wool. It was not the sea of rest. It was the sea of judgment.

The clan moved slowly, each step deliberate. It seemed so long ago when Toddy had found feathers strewn among the roots of a fallen tree. Weather and time have left their mark on each one: black, white, and ash-gray. She gathered them, placed them in her pouch, and instantly knew that someday they would have meaning.

Brindle, more like a ram than a lamb, painted with streaked wool and quiet eyes, watched her. He didn't blink. He circled a windswept tree once, then lay beside it.

Kara saw it as a sign. "Hold on to them," she said. "The wind waits for us."

Toddy kept her feathers in a pouch she had fashioned from Brindle's wool and held it close to her chest.

It was not long before they came across the Salt Clan, who had created a homestead in a hollow, carved out of the dune by wind and time. There were no walls. No gates. Inside their makeshift shelter, they had a fire that burned without smoke.

The people wore cloaks made of seaweed and sinew. Salt lines, ritual scars, ran across their faces, glowing in the fading light.

They were greeted by a woman who called herself Sela. She spoke to them in a low, rough voice, like sand beneath water. "You carry the wind." She said. Kara nodded. "It carries us."

Sela looked at Toddy. "And the girl speaks to it?"

Toddy blinked. "I hear you."

Sela smiled. "Then you are welcome."

The Salt Clan asked no questions. They offered drink and fire. They spoke in fragments—half-remembered warnings, songs without tunes.

Kara listened. Lance paid close attention. Toddy was lost in her words.

She saw a spiral carved into the stone that was full of feathers and bones. "What is this?" she asked.

Sela said to her. "It's a doorway."

"A doorway?" Toddy asked.

“For the wind.” Sela said. “So that it may hear our dreams.”

Toddy knelt beside the totem. She placed one of her feathers in the spiral. “I dreamed of the sea,” she said softly.

The wind blew salt and sand across the shelter’s opening. The sheep were restless that night.

Brindle walked around the fire three times before lying down. Thorn refused to sleep. Moss bleated once, then wandered off. Echo and Rook stood nearby.

At dawn, Kara found Thorn standing on the ridge above the hollow.

He wasn’t alone.

There was a figure next to him, tall and wearing a cloak made of seal skins that had been stained with salt. Kara approached slowly.

“Who are you?” she asked.

The figure wasn’t a person. It was shaped by the wind. A memory. A warning. It said, “You named me.”
Kara swallowed. “The hunger.”

The figure nodded. “And now I call you.”

Whatever it was, it put a hand on her chest. “Keeper.” Then it vanished. The clan met at the spiral, the center of it all; Toddy stood with feathers in her hands. Lance stood next to her, clenching his ever-present knife. Kara stood at the edge, her spear on the ground.

Sela spoke. "The wind has made its choice."

Toddy looked up. "Is it our line of mothers?"

Sela smiled, "No. It's older."

Toddy placed the feathers in the spiral. "We give it a name," she said. "We give it food. We hear."

The wind moved again. Echo made a noise. And the spiral sang.

The Salt Clan didn't say goodbye. They just turned away from them and looked at the sea.

Brindle followed Toddy. Moss was now making his way, walking at a leisurely pace. Thorn was in charge. Echo followed Kara. Rook returned, quiet and watchful.

The wind came after. Kara said nothing. But she wouldn't forget.

Chapter 22

The Marsh

They arrived at the salt marsh at dawn.

It was like a mirror with reeds and still pools, distorting the illusion of reality. The ground was soft and dangerous. Sound traveled strangely, with echoes bending and whispers getting lost. Fog blurred the edges, as if it were cautioning them.

Toddy moved forward, closing her eyes, listening for guidance. “I hear it,” she said. Lance hesitated. “What does it say?”

Toddy turned her head. “It whispers to me. It’s waiting.”

The child led the way; the clan trailed behind her in a line. Brindle lost her footing; Moss clung to Kara’s shadow. Thorn jumped from tuft to tuft. Echo bleated, unsure. Rook walked without fear.

The wind wasn’t leading them; it was testing them.

In the fog, a shape moved; it was not a monster. Not a person. It observed.

Toddy stopped. “It’s here.” Lance pulled out his knife. Kara held up her spear.

The shape didn't say anything.

Toddy moved forward. "You listen too," she said.

The shape was gone. They got to the far bank at dusk. The wind was calm. Toddy turned around. "It's not gone." She said. "It's watching."

Chapter 23

The Drowned Grove

They encountered a grove of trees that grew along the edges of the marsh. It was midday.

They were never warned about any dangers in the marsh trees. The trees grew out of brackish water, and their roots twisted like sleeping snakes. The air was thick with rot and bloom. Red petals floated on the surface, like drops of blood.

The clan hesitated. The wind paused.

Toddy stepped forward. “It’s listening again.”

Kara nodded. “It always does.” They walked between the trees, careful not to disturb the water. Echo bleated once and then fell silent. Thorn sniffed the air.

Moss stayed close to Brindle. Rook was gone.

A voice came from the grove. Not words. It was not a song. A shaking.

Kara knelt. She placed her hand in the water. “It knows we’re here.”

The trees responded. The leaves shifted. The petals fell.

A small, hunched figure emerged, covered in vines. Its face was bark. It had no eyes. "You have names," it said.

Kara nodded. "We have stories."

The figure reached out. "Then put them in the water."

Kara opened her bag. She placed feathers, salt, and a piece of spiral stone into the water.

The grove sparkled.

Kara stepped back. Lance put down his knife. Thorn lay down. Echo bleated once again.

Kara rose. "It's getting bigger."

They lingered. Toddy walked along the edge of the grove, touching the trees. She put salt on one trunk, and then another. "This place will remember us," she said.

She faced Kara and asked. "Will it help us find our land?"

Kara looked toward the ridge. "It already has." They put their things together. Rook came back, but he was quiet. Moss rubbed against Toddy's hand, seeking comfort.

As they left, the grove shook once, sending a wave across the water.

Kara didn't look back. She was in charge.

The water sang behind them. The wind waited.

The search continued. The wolves disappeared over a rise some distance away.

Chapter 24

The Crossing

They left the broken coast without any fanfare. No spirals. No feathers. No words. The only sound that could be heard was the crunch of stone beneath their feet and the weight of silence between them.

The wind had stopped blowing, but it was still there, just no longer important. Kara didn't listen for it. She listened to the beat of her steps.

The land changed. Hills rose, dried, and sunburned. The sea shrank and then curved away. They followed a path shaped by time and erosion, not prophecy.

Toddy walked beside Kara, eyes open yet unfocused. Kale followed, hands wrapped in old cloth. He carried nothing but thoughts.

"We've been chasing echoes," Kara said.

Toddy nodded. "And now?" Kara looked ahead.

"We build a new tomorrow." Drud grunted softly, "Stone remembers. But it doesn't let go."

Kale has become more aware, not just of the world but also of the thread that connected them to it. "Then we shape it," he said. "We do not worship it."

It wasn't defiance. It was clarity. A statement: Reality is not a temple to kneel before but clay to shape with the fire of conscience.

They got to a ridge that looked out over a green, fertile, terraced valley. There was smoke coming from distant hearths.

Not ruins. Not remnants. Life.

Drud stepped forward. "Do you think they're like us?"

Kara shook her head. "They're people, like us."

They descended slowly.

The valley wasn't quiet, but it wasn't loud. Children watched from behind olive trees. Elders stood in the doorways. There was no one who spoke. Kara approached the nearest shelter. A man stood outside with his arms crossed, eyes wary.

"We're not here to take," she said. "We're here to start."

The man looked her over. "You don't carry anything."

Kara opened her bag. Salt, stone, feathers, and obsidian. She put them on the ground. "We carry memories," she said. "But we're done worshiping them."

Toddy moved forward. Wise beyond her years, she said, "We want to learn."

Sang lowered her head. “We want to earn our place.”

Drud put a stone next to Kara’s. “We want to stay.”

The man nodded once. “Then you'll work.”

And they did.

Sang tended the sheep. Drud gathered herbs and watched over the fields. Kale built walls.

Toddy instructed the children. Kara paid attention to the people. Not to the wind. Not to omens.

The clan didn’t go away. They became part of the valley, its work, its laughter, its rhythm, and its people.

They didn’t preach; they told them stories. They planted their history. The spiral was no longer a shrine; it was a tool.

One night, Kara stood on the ridge. The stars were bright. The wind was calm. Toddy joined her. “Do you miss your past?”

Kara shook her head. “It was never meant to last.”

Toddy smiled. “But we were.”

The valley breathed below them. Their future before them. Her final thought: to wean herself and her clan. Rituals they worried over hadn’t helped them in their darkest hours. What got them this far was determination.

Epilogue

The First Garden

The land didn't send them away.

It didn't test them, call them by name, or speak in riddles. It simply opened, soft soil, clean water, patient trees.

The empty coast held them like a palm holds a seed. And this time, they didn't ask to stay.

They worked tirelessly. Used stone to build. Instead of creating spirals, they constructed walls; instead of alters, they grew new gardens.

Toddy planted herbs she'd never seen before. Sang learned how to laugh. Drud taught the children how to hunt. Kale made terraces with calm hands. Kara quietly made tools out of driftwood.

The lambs roamed freely. Moss nestled among the thyme; Thorn lingered near the orchard, and Echo watched her young. Brindle circled the hearth, keeping time with the fire.

Kara walked around the edge of their new home every morning. Not to protect, but to greet. She no longer listened for the wind. She heard footsteps and laughter. It was the sound of something to protect. Their memories will guide them.

They thrived, not because the land was easy, but because they were honest with it. They stopped looking for signs. They made choices. If they failed, then they tried again.

The joy came quietly.

Toddy smiled when she bit into a fig during the first harvest.

Sang tapped out rhythms no one had taught her during the night dances. Kara didn't tell the children what happened in the stories anymore; she told them what could happen.

They didn't become new people by magic. They worked diligently to become one with their new home. They listened to their inner selves. By naming themselves.

Even after they settled, one question remained: What would they face now that the land had accepted them?

The answer wasn't the stars, the wind, or the soil. The answer lay in the children, who would remember their hunger and the efforts required to overcome their trials.

Who would ask new questions?

Who would build not on what was lost, but on what could be done?

Kara knew that this moment was the real beginning.

From atop a tall rise, Bing and his pack would watch their friends far below. The wolf pack went unseen for several moon cycles, but Toddy visited the hills to be near them. When they followed her home, their presence soon disrupted their new clan's routine. How was it possible to walk with wolves?

Made in the USA
Coppell, TX
21 June 2026

83020328R00049